# A Fairy-Tale Day

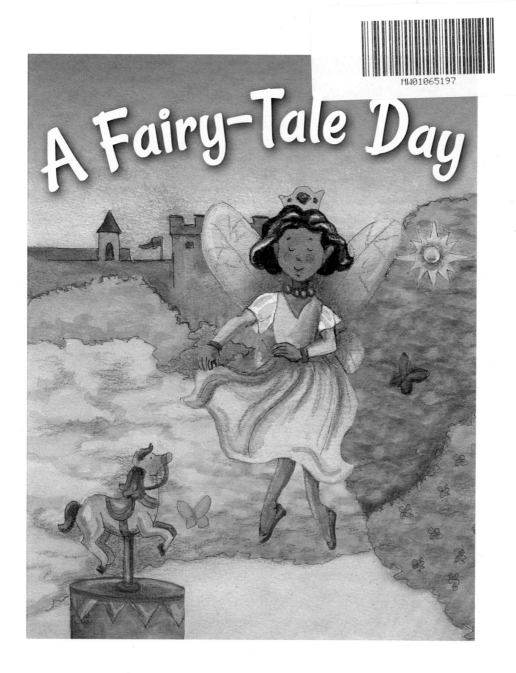

## By Dani Neiley
## Illustrated by Dee S. Kent

MW01065197

I need to eat.

I need to play.

I need to dance.

I need to wave.

I need to fly!

I need to help.

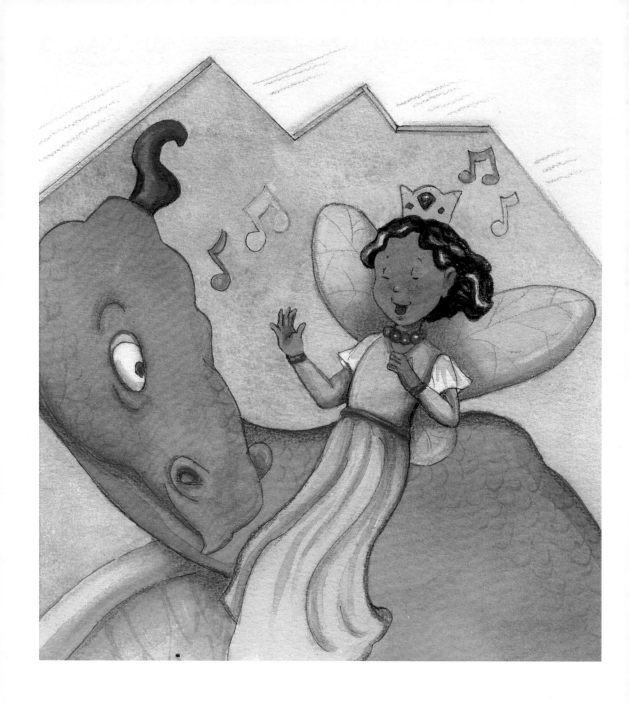

I need to sing.

I need to bow.

I need to go.

I need to sleep.

**Publishing Credits**

Rachelle Cracchiolo, M.S.Ed., *Publisher*
Conni Medina, M.A.Ed., *Editor in Chief*
Nika Fabienke, Ed.D., *Content Director*
Véronique Bos, *Creative Director*
Shaun Bernadou, *Art Director*
Stephanie Loureiro, *Associate Editor*
Jess Johnson, *Graphic Designer*

**Image Credits:** Illustrations by Dee S. Kent.

**Library of Congress Cataloging-in-Publication Data**

Names: Neiley, Dani, author. | Kent, Dee S., illustrator.
Title: A fairytale day / by Dani Neiley ; illustrated by Dee S. Kent.
Other titles: A fairy tale day
Description: Huntington Beach, CA : Teacher Created Materials, 2019. |
   Summary: "What does a fairy princess do in a day? Find out!"-- Provided by
   publisher.
Identifiers: LCCN 2019014338 | ISBN 9781644913055 (pbk.)
Subjects: | CYAC: Fairies--Fiction. | Princesses--Fiction.
Classification: LCC PZ7.1.N397 Fai 2019 | DDC [E]--dc23 LC record available
at https://lccn.loc.gov/2019014338

**TCM** | Teacher Created Materials

5301 Oceanus Drive
Huntington Beach, CA 92649-1030
www.tcmpub.com
**ISBN 978-1-6449-1305-5**
© 2020 Teacher Created Materials, Inc.